The Selkie Chronicles

Ara's Prelude

Companion Tales for
Ara's Song

D. August Baertlein

Dedication

For all creatures born ultimately from the sea,
large or small,
scaled, feathered, or finned,
human or non.

Contents

Introduction

S elkies, Sylkies, Selchies, *Kópakonan*. The Seal Folk go by many names, all given to them by clueless humans describing this noble race as unsubstantiated cryptids like the Yeti, Chupacabra, or Loch Ness Monster. To further complicate matters, mythologies from time immemorial have confused Selkies with Merfolk, Merrow, Finfolk, and Kelpies. But these seal shapeshifters are infinitely superior to any furry, scaled, or horse-type fantasy. For one thing, they're real.

You've seen Selkies, I'm sure, in videos at the very least. But the best way to spot them is from a small boat along a rocky coast. Catching sight of their sleek, dark bodies gliding through the water as salt air stings your face—now that's an experience nothing short of magical. And if you're really fortunate, one will angle up an eye brimming with intelligence and curiosity. When your gazes lock, the electric arc that passes between you and this amazing creature will leave you no doubt. You've just met a Selkie.

Selkies may look like ordinary sea lions and seals, but they are enchanted beings. They shed their sealskins on moonlit nights, revealing human forms more magnificent than imaginable. Their shapes, male and female alike, are so beautiful that, dancing across the sand like spirits born of wind and wave, they hold any soul that sees them spellbound.

As a courtesy to us weak-willed land folk, Selkies make every effort to hide their midnight dances, for gods preserve any man or woman enchanted by a Selkie's unwitting allure, seduced by the sight, song, and smell of these remarkable creatures.

And gods preserve the Selkie, too, when a covetous human abducts one of these glorious creatures of the sea to hold as a captive on dry land.

***

The short stories in this book, *Ara's Prelude:*

Companion Tales for Ara's Song, appear chronologically, but each one also stands alone. If you find them intriguing, you may want to check out the further adventures of these characters in the novel *Ara's Song* in *The Selkie Chronicles* series.

In ordinary time, *Ara's Song* begins after *Ara's Prelude* ends, but nothing would be missed or spoiled if the order of the books was transposed. These characters and their tales overlap like ripples in a pond. They propagate beyond the pages of these books. In truth, stories never end if storytellers are encouraged to write on.

So, if you enjoy *Ara's Prelude*, it would greatly help the author for you to leave a review wherever you bought this book.

Chapter 1:
Cadence and the Selkie

It was binding, Cadence supposed, now that the marriage was consummated. No chance of backing out, if ever there had been. The bachelor pool on Lítill Vanta Island was minuscule, and her parents had jumped at the good pastor's offer to take her off their hands, though he was twice her seventeen years. She wondered if this was even legal, but folks did as they pleased out here in the middle of the North Atlantic.

The cottage's front door clicked as Reverend Silas Lockheart hurried off to another church duty, this one on a Tuesday afternoon. How much time did it take to prepare one lousy sermon a week? It was as if he could barely stand the sight of her, the way he was never home. It'd taken an entire month for him to get around to this husbandly duty, not that she minded. He could take all the time he wanted if this was all there was in it for her.

She rolled off the eiderdown bed and pulled her skirt back down over her thighs. A walk might clear her mind, but the walk she craved wasn't meant for skirts. So she changed into jeans and sneakers, swept her hair into a claw clip, and slung a backpack of water and snacks over her shoulder.

The public path from the front door of Lockheart's house—her house now, too—led uphill to Morgan's Market and Petra's Pub, the only two commercial establishments on the island. There was a small schoolhouse past those, but she didn't walk as far as any of them before taking the gently used sheep's path on the left. She followed it up a grassy incline, greeting her father's ram and four ewes with pats to the head. She missed them terribly, but Lockheart had deemed working with beasts beneath her status as the pastor's wife.

When the path gave way to solid rock, she found the familiar hand and toeholds leading to her favorite cliffside perch overlooking the ocean. Standing there, wind in her face, she willed her breath to slow, to match the waves beating against the rocks below. Gulls soared overhead. Petrels skimmed the sea, dipping now and again to snag a fish. A lone seal barked.

All of them were free, and here she was, a matron at seventeen. It was bloody unfair.

She set her knapsack on a grassy hillock back away from the cliff's sharp edge and extracted a zippered bag. From this, she pulled three parts and assembled them into an alto recorder, the wood of it warm to her touch. Stepping to the very edge of the cliff, she lowered herself to a familiar small bowl in the rock that fit her bum as if it were made for it.

When she put the worn mouthpiece to her lips and played, what came out was not so much a tune as a melancholy string of notes, an impromptu dirge, maybe. The requiem flowed from her heart to her lungs and out through the instrument as easily as water from a spring, and she played for several minutes, hoping music would lift her spirits.

It didn't.

When tears made it hard to play, she put down the recorder and let the droplets trace paths down her cheeks, drip off her chin, and fall into the sea.

The seal barked again, and she peered over

the cliff's edge to where he floated just below, looking up at her as though he'd been there all along, listening.

"Oh, yeah?" She wiped her nose with the back of her hand. "Well, everyone's a critic." The truth was, she was glad for the company. "Shall I try something more upbeat?"

He nodded two quick dips of his chin, whether in answer or just to scratch an itch, she couldn't know. But she took up her pipe and played "The Queen of All Argyll." By the time she reached the closing bar, she did feel a little better. The seal, swimming lazy spirals below, cheered her even more.

But the sun was sinking, and she was responsible for her husband's supper these days. She'd pick up a loaf of rye from the market to go with the crock-pot of mutton stew she'd left simmering.

***

An extreme low tide came early the following day. Cadence took her bucket and short-handled rake to the only stretch of beach on Lítill Vanta and was bent over digging clams and dropping the mud-caked gems into her bucket when a black shadow offshore caught her eye. A seal, heading straight for this very stretch of coastline.

It was odd to see one without its pod, but, like the afternoon before, this fellow appeared to swim solo. She raised a hand to her brow, shielding her eyes for a better look. A dollop of mud skittered down her face and onto her shirt. Cursing under her breath, she tried to brush it off but managed only to smear it worse. Not that it mattered. These were work clothes; they'd seen dirt before and would again.

By the time she looked up, the seal had dragged himself up the beach to within meters of her. He didn't flop down and take a nap as was customary for seals in these parts. He just sat there, head high, watching her.

"If you're expecting another concert," she said. "I didn't bring my recorder." She went back to raking, wondering if this could possibly be the same seal from the day before.

The animal hauled closer and peered into her bucket.

"You hungry?" She tossed him a clam, which he wallowed in his mouth, then spit back with an easy arc into her bucket.

"Not a fan?" She sat back on her heels. "Honestly, I'm not either. But the good reverend loves a good chowder, so here I—"

"What the devil has gotten into you?" In a

flash, Reverend Silas Lockheart had her by the collar, lifting her to standing. How he'd snuck up on the both of them, she couldn't fathom.

"No wife of mine will be seen wallowing in the mud," he said, dragging her up the beach. "Purity is a state of body as well as mind."

"But the clams…" she said, turning back for the bucket.

"Forget them."

His grip was uncompromising.

***

When Cadence got out of the shower, Silas was in his ugly plaid easy chair in the living room, sipping claret and waiting for her.

"Sit," he ordered.

She hadn't made it to the bedroom to dress yet, so she cinched the towel tighter around her chest, tucked one leg under herself in the chair across from him, and returned his glare.

"I trust you understand where things stand?"

"Well, that's very trusting of you," she said, though she felt she understood nothing. She'd thought she had some idea of what marriage was about from novels and what few movies made it out here to the middle of the ocean. Even watching her parents, she'd seen a modicum of affection between them. What this was, she had no idea.

Lockheart let out a slow breath of false patience. "You," he said, "are now in a position of moral authority. You are the wife of this community's religious leader. I'm practically their god," he said. "Which makes you..." He waved his hand as if either it went without saying, or he didn't know himself.

"I..." She faltered. "I'm the same Cadence Marie Ashland that everyone on this island has known from birth. I've been digging clams since I was six, sheering sheep since I was eight, and climbing cliffs since I could walk. If that displeases you, why in God's name did you choose me for your wife?"

Lockheart winced at her use of God's name, but he didn't respond. He didn't need to. If the bachelor pool on Lítill Vanta was small, the maiden pool was smaller still. She, it was suddenly clear, was only meant to buy him respectability. And she was failing at that.

"Look," she said. "I'm willing to be reasonable—not curse, attend church every Sunday, not sleep around."

He winced again.

"Okay." She raised both palms in a gesture of placation. "Not even talk of sleeping around. But I'm still me. You can't take that away."

His lips pursed as though he were thinking it over.

"I only wanted to get you a good supper. Isn't that worth something? Everyone knows you love clam chowder."

He placed his empty glass on the end table and rose. "Supper will be at the pub."

"Great." She sprung up and headed for the bedroom. "Give me a minute to dress."

"Not you." He felt in his jacket pocket for his glasses, placed them on his nose, and walked to the door. "You will spend the evening praying on your choices. By the time I return, I hope you'll have come to your senses."

And he was gone.

"Stupid, effing, north-end-of-a-south-going-mule!" She stomped to the bedroom and pulled her favorite pair of overalls from the last of her moving boxes, the one Lockheart had suggested she burn.

She was sitting cross-legged on the couch with a bowl of leftover mutton stew in her lap when there came a scrabbling at the door.

"Back already?" she mumbled but didn't get up.

When the scratching had gone on long enough to be irritating, she slammed her bowl on the end table and went to the door. "What is your damned problem?" she said as she swung it open.

But it wasn't her husband. This man was taller, younger, bare-chested, and totally unfamiliar. Everyone knew everyone on the island, so where had this stranger come from? He held out an offering, but she was too busy falling into those bottomless, coal-black eyes to see what it was. So, he pressed a handle into her grip.

The rank smell of it finally made her look down to find that she was holding her clam bucket. It contained a dozen muddy clams, now oozing death. She gagged and darted around the man to set it outside. Thinking better of leaving it beside the front door, she carried it to a spot out behind the garden wall.

When she turned to go back to the house, the man was directly behind her. Now that he'd rid himself of the bucket, she could see that his chest was not his only bare part. And he seemed quite comfortable with nudity.

"Thank you?" she said, then blushed to think he might not understand she was referring to the bucket, not the view he was providing.

***

9

She probably shouldn't have let him in that night. Or the fourteen nights that followed. But he seemed positively God-sent. Reverend Lockheart went out to the pub every evening to "keep in touch with his parishioners." He stayed away for hours while Cadence was left to her own devices.

The first night, she gave the stranger a pair of ridiculous striped pants that Lockheart would never miss and a cup of tea that the man sniffed but wouldn't drink. He said very little, she realized afterwards, but was content to let her do all the talking. And he listened. She could tell by his eyes and the inscrutable smile that never left his face. This was such a rarity that she basked in it.

When prodded, he gave his name as Tatzeek, which sounded vaguely Arabic. But the few words he spoke seemed crafted to mimic her accent rather than stem from anything she'd ever heard. So she had no clue where he'd come from or where he went each night when she sent him off just before Lockheart was likely to return.

Cadence looked for Tatzeek during the days, of course—in the market or at the dock. She even checked the pub once or twice, but she never spoke of him to anyone. And no one ever mentioned a tall, dark-eyed stranger, with or without Lockheart's striped pants.

Over those two weeks, Tatzeek began to speak more freely, and his knowledge of the sea fascinated her. They often engaged in absurd games of charades before she could figure out precisely what he was talking about. He did a fantastic jellyfish, arms all akimbo, and his humpback whale breaching onto the couch was picture perfect.

On the fifteenth night, she told him she loved him. On the sixteenth, he confessed to the same, and though there was no marriage to consummate, they consummated anyway.

"Oh my!" Cadence spread her arms across Lockheart's high, feather bed. "Now I see what all the fuss is about."

Tatzeek sat up and put his head in his hands.

"What's wrong?" she said. "Did I not do it right? We can try again."

"No." He laughed, but it was not the airy laugh from his heart that she had come to love. "It is I who have done wrong."

"I can't imagine," she said breathlessly.

He took her hands in his. "I have not been true with you, my Cadence." When she opened her mouth to contradict him, he put a finger to her lips. "I am not what you think."

"I haven't figured out what to think," she

said. "So, I doubt you've lied." But she pulled her hands away, prepared for the worst. Or so she thought.

"I am Selkie," he said.

She snorted disbelief. "You mean a seal person?"

Then her mind played out the evidence as she sat up in bed and gathered the sheets around her.

There was that friendly, black-eyed seal from clam-digging day, and the bucket Tatzeek had returned. There was his initial nakedness, and the fact that now he wore only the pants she'd given him. Every single night the same pants. And no shoes. And how else could she explain his vast knowledge of creatures of the deep?

"Yes." He nodded. "I am Prince Tatzeek of the Seal people."

"Ohhh—kay," Cadence drew the word out, giving herself time to think. "That's not so bad, I guess." She leaned in and kissed his cheek.

"Also." Tatzeek dipped his chin to watch her from beneath thick brows. "I am mated to a seal-woman destined to become my Selkie queen," he said quickly, as though he'd practiced it a hundred times.

"Oh!"

"But I do not love her." He reached for

Cadence's hands. "I love only you."

Her gaze flitted around the room for something solid to land on and found the bedside clock.

"Oh my God!" She jumped from the bed and gathered her clothes. "Get out!" she yelled, tossing him his pants.

"I am so sorry, Cadence. I—"

"Go!" She spun him toward the door and gave him a shove. "Quickly. Before my husband returns!"

So Prince Tatzeek of the Seal People slipped out the back door only seconds before the latch clicked on the front.

***

Tatzeek returned, as usual, the next night. Cadence wasn't sure he would, and she wasn't sure she wanted him to. But she had questions, even after reading all she could on the subject of Selkies, which amounted to a chapter in the book *Myths and Legends the Church Must Dispel* that stood on Reverend Lockheart's bookshelf.

At Tatzeek's knocking, she flung wide the door. "So," she said, turning her back on him. "Am I enchanted, then? Bedazzled by your stupid Selkie spell?" When she got to the parlor, she tucked her leg under herself and

13

plopped into Silas's favorite chair, the one he liked to pontificate from.

"I thought it was love I felt." She tapped the book she'd left laying open on the coffee table. "But so did they."

Tatzeek eyed the drawing of a girl half out of her sealskin, mid-transformation. "I do not know if it's a spell," he said. "You are my first human."

"Well, *that* makes me feel better."

He smiled as only one not yet schooled in sarcasm would. "But I am most certain you are not enchanted."

"And why is that?"

"You are strong of spirit, Cadence. And..." He paused, studying her. "I think you could not be so angry with me were you under my spell."

She raised an eyebrow. "Then maybe a better question is, 'Did you *intend* to enchant me?'"

"Of course, no!" He sat on the edge of the chair closest to her. "The Selkie spell is never cast on purpose. We are just very... attractive."

That he was. Even now, when she wanted to hate him, she couldn't quite manage it. It worried her how quickly her anger was fading.

Then she remembered the wife, and it flared. "So, why are you here, Tatzeek? A married man. What made you come to me in the first place, if not to ensnare me?"

His mouth twitched into a bewildered smile, and his eyes grew distant. "That I do not know," he said. "It is very strange how much you drew me. It happened that first day we met."

"On the beach?"

"No. The late-day before. You were high up on the cliff making song sounds." He mimed putting a recorder to his lips.

"That *was* you." She had thought so.

"Your…" He traced a line down his cheek, searching for the word.

"Tears?"

"Yes, tears. They fell on me. I think it might be humans have a magic, too."

Wasn't that just like a man to put the blame back on the woman? Which reminded her. "Tell me about this wife you don't love."

It seemed Tatzeek's aging father had forced him into a mating bond. The king wanted to ensure his heir had a successor of his own before some catastrophe befell him. A Selkie's natural life might be a hundred years or more, but sharks, seal hunters, and natural disasters could cut that short. As crown prince, Tatzeek had responsibilities.

Cadence and Tatzeek walked hand-in-hand to the shore that night, leaving well before

Lockheart would return. Tatzeek led her down a little-used path away from town, where no one would be out so late. At the base of the cliff, as soft waves shushed against the sand, he kissed her cheek.

He pulled a fuzzy, brown wad from between the rocks. Taking off Lockheart's ugly striped pants, he tucked them where his sealskin had been hidden and walked to the water's edge. Knee-deep in surging waves, he pressed the pelt to his calf, and it came alive.

As it squirmed up his leg to cover his body, she realized they weren't so different, she and Tatzeek. Both married against their will. Both swapping skins to fit into a world where they didn't belong.

"Will you be back?" she asked.

"If you will have me," he replied.

Her smile was all the answer he needed to bring him back night after night for many moons to come. Which isn't exactly the same as happily ever after.

Chapter 2:
The Trade

Fiona's friends thought she was completely mental, taking a newborn aboard a commercial fishing boat. But for her and Colin, it was the only choice. Fiona wasn't just Colin's wife; she was his first mate, and, as he liked to joke, she worked cheap to boot.

Anyway, they couldn't afford a nanny, what with house and boat payments. It turned out fishing the North Atlantic wasn't all that lucrative. It was a good life, though, at least to begin with.

Fiona told anyone who'd listen that Seamus was the perfect sea-baby. While she and Colin worked, he slept in the cradle they'd fixed to the floor of the boat's wheelhouse. And even when the ocean pitched the *Seabreeze* higher than Fiona would have liked, Seamus woke laughing and begging for more.

The bairn was more at home at sea than on dry land and especially enjoyed their encounters with seals. At least one pod showed up most days, and sometimes a group of the seadogs followed the boat for hours. Probably because they were after the same thing Colin and Fiona were—a school of fat herring.

But by his second summer, Seamus insisted on spending more and more time awake and out on deck, and Fiona had to work out ways to manage the little rapscallion.

She'd ordered a front-loading baby carrier from the mainland, which freed her hands to work. But she hadn't bothered to use it this day. Coiling the tie-line would take only a moment, and she figured she could work one-handed for that long. But Fiona hadn't counted on the arrival of Seamus's best friend.

"Goggy!" he yelled, scrambling for the seal pup now fliping summersaults in the air off the lee side of the boat.

A split second before Seamus tumbled overboard, Fiona juggled her babe into a secure football hold. "No, love," she said, quashing her fear under a layer of normalcy. "Not Doggy. Seely."

This wasn't the first time he'd mistaken one for kin to the sheepdog that slept at the foot of his bed. "That's a sealy, dear."

Seamus wrinkled his wee brow. After a few tries, he came out with a delighted screech of "Eely!" and the pup pirouetted like a show pony, apparently pleased with its new name.

Eely came around almost every day after that. If Fiona couldn't tell one seal from another, Seamus sure could. "Eely!" he'd cry, and the pup would prove him right by flipping a fancy dive that revealed its distinctive, heart-shaped white scar.

Fiona sometimes tossed a herring for the little seal, though Colin disapproved. "They're not pets," he'd say. "We can't afford to feed the lot of them." But even Colin began to look forward to the pup's arrival. "Have you seen Shaymie's girlfriend yet?" he'd tease.

They'd remember those happy times fondly, but nothing lasts forever.

It was just a typical foggy morning when Seamus was nearly two. The *Seabreeze* was an hour out of port with Colin at the helm and Fiona playing pat-a-cake with the rambunctious toddler.

"Maybe some fresh air will take the spunk

out of him," Colin suggested. They needed him worn out by the time they got too busy with the nets to keep track of the boy.

Fiona shrugged. "It's worth a try." She scooped Seamus from the playpen that was now fixed where his cradle had been and carried him out on deck.

She braced against the wheelhouse to shelter them both from the strongest wind, and they set to scanning the area. Fiona looked for signs of fish—dark patches in the water or a flock of feeding seabirds. Seamus had eyes only for Eely.

Colin shouted first. "Fishes ho!" he called and re-aimed the *Seabreeze* toward a flock of diving gulls. "Herring, I'll wager!" His voice held the same swell of excitement Seamus used for an Eely sighting, and Fiona smiled at the father/son resemblance.

She kissed the toddler's curly head and braced her hip against the gunwale to lean into the *Seabreeze's* sharp turn. Once they'd straightened, she made her way back to the cabin and set Seamus into his playpen.

"I'll take the wheel," she said, though her child was howling dismay at his sudden imprisonment.

Colin scampered aft to secure their purse net to the overhead pulley run by a diesel-powered winch. Fiona maneuvered the boat up beside where the feeding gulls dive-bombed the water. As quickly as a bird popped up and swallowed a fish, it would take to the sky for another dive. Something was driving the herring up from below, too, into the bird's feeding frenzy. A shark, maybe?

Fiona couldn't help but pity the doomed fish as she watched Colin prepare to encircle them from the sides as well, effectively blocking their last escape.

But her family had to eat, too. So, she judged the wind and current, and positioned the boat to advantage, then nodded to her husband, signaling him to drop the first edge of the net. Floats held its top flush with the surface while weights pulled the bottom down like curtain-fall at the end of a play—the final act for hundreds of fish.

She steered the *Seabreeze* in an arc around the school as Colin fed out the net. When she'd brought them full circle, she idled the boat so Colin could fasten the net's ends together. Then he pulled the cable to gather the bottom edge like the mouth of a purse.

Her helmsman's tasks completed, Fiona pulled a stuffed seal from Seamus's toy bag in the corner. "Have a rest, love," she said, waving its well-chewed tail at the child. "I need to help Da for a bit."

But Seamus didn't reach for the trifle. His fists gripped the rail of his baby jail, and he glared as if to say, *Hang your stupid toy and let me out of here.*

"Fiona?" Colin called. "Whenever you're ready." The forced calm in his voice unnerved Fiona.

She tossed the toy at Seamus's feet and dashed out of the wheelhouse, scanning for trouble as she ran. They'd netted a fine mess of herring, but for some reason, the hoist motor was silent. The net hung in place, its top rim hanging barely above the water.

"What's wrong?" she said, expecting that the motor had died. But Colin pointed to a spot across the way where water splashed, frantic beyond the norm for agitated fish.

"What is it?" She moved to the railing for a better look just as a black flipper slapped the surface. A small, black tail with a white, heart-shaped scar.

"Eely!" she cried. It must have been the pup driving the fish from below. Now it was snagged in their net.

Fiona grabbed for the remote in Colin's hand, the one that controlled the winch. "Pull her up!" she yelled. "She's drowning!"

Colin swung the remote over Fiona's head,

out of her reach. "It's too heavy," he said. "Either the winch will burn out, or the net will rip."

His jaw tensed as he watched the animal struggle, and his eyes wouldn't meet Fiona's. "Anyway," he said. "She'll figure it out. I heard seals can hold their breaths for an hour."

"Even the babies?"

Colin shrugged.

One of the pup's pectoral fins protruded through a loop in the mesh while its head squirmed out another. It was held fast underwater. The more the animal wriggled, the tighter the net pinched.

Fiona cupped her hands over her face. "We have to do something!" Her mind raced. "Maybe lift the net enough so she can breathe while she works her way out?"

"I tried that."

Colin made no move, so Fiona reached again for the remote. "We can't just—"

"Fiona." He turned on her. "Folks on the island hunt seal pups for their skins all the time. You know that. Right over there on that nursery beach." He waved toward Lítill Vanta, where they'd made their home for the last several years. "It's not like this pup is anything special."

But she was. She was Eely. Shaymie's

23

girlfriend.

The pup's cries rose, muffled by the water but audible. Little Seamus heard it too, and his sobs from the playpen made a mournful harmony.

"But she's so frightened, Colin." Fiona touched his arm.

"Well, I'm bloody petrified," he said. Fiona could see it in his face. "Every single night when I'm trying to sleep. Afraid we'll starve if we can't make a go of it, if we can't pay off the boat before they foreclose." He waved to where the hoist was stalled. "We can't afford a new winch. Or a new net, for that matter."

Decisively, he turned on his heel and strode to the cabin, returning with the pistol they kept for emergencies.

But surely this wasn't an emergency. "Colin, no!" She grabbed for the gun. But he was tall, and his arms were too long for her to reach.

"You got a better idea? This way we could put the animal out of its misery, sell the skin, and feed the meat to the dogs."

"The net would still be too heavy for the winch," she argued. "A seal weighs as much dead as alive."

"We'll drag it alongside the boat. At least dead it won't be fighting, suffering, and ripping things all to hell."

Dragging a net rather than hauling it aboard was not unheard of. That was how fishermen in better times dealt with a super huge catch. Needless to say, Colin and Fiona had never had reason to try it.

She dredged her brain for a better idea as the pup's bleats weakened.

A few hundred yards out, something rose in the water. A seal. Adult female, by the size and shape of her head. She shot toward them, arching out of the water, porpoise-style, like a needle weaving a seam of froth straight at the *Seabreeze*.

Colin, still focused on the pup, lifted the pistol and took aim.

"Wait!" Fiona pushed the gun aside. "Maybe she can help." She pointed to the seal, now nearly there.

"Or wreak more havoc." But Colin lowered his arm.

Fiona gently took the remote from his other hand. "We could help her a little." She checked to see that it was set to UP, then flicked it on. But the winch only screamed and strained. The net shuddered but wouldn't rise, and the motor started to smoke, so she turned it off.

The adult seal was at the pup's side now, outside the net. She bit and tore, but it wouldn't give.

Fiona pulled a pocketknife from her jeans. Rolled it over in her hand. Opened it, shut it, and opened it again.

"What'll you do with that?" Colin said. It might have been a taunt except for the hope she detected in his voice.

But she had no plan. She was a decent swimmer, but that water was like ice. She'd never make it there and back, let alone have time to cut through the net and free the pup in between.

A dripping sound broke into her consciousness, and only then did she notice how quiet Seamus had become. All was silent except for the frantic splashing in front of her and that drip, drip, drip behind. What was it?

Fiona turned to find a man standing at the boat's railing—wet, muscular, and very naked. Unable to look away, she raised a hand to her gaping mouth. He was gorgeous with longish honey-blond hair and a cloud-like beard to match. And every part of him was mantled in muscle so flawless he could have been a work of art.

A statue.

Perfection.

"What the..." Colin was less impressed. "Put the child down!" he demanded.

Child? The man stood in a trail of water

extending from the side of the boat to the wheelhouse. In the crook of one arm, he cradled Seamus much as Fiona had earlier, the only difference being, he held the boy out over the side of the boat.

Seamus wasn't concerned, though. In fact, he seemed enraptured as he gazed into the man's unnaturally black eyes and wove his little fingers through the man's dripping beard

"Trade," the man said with an accent unfamiliar to Fiona.

Colin dropped the remote and raised his pistol, aiming with both hands now. "Put. The. Lad. Down," he said as if it were four one-word sentences.

The man raised an eyebrow, pointedly looking to the sea yawning beneath the baby's feet.

"Fine, fine!" Colin said. "You're right. Don't drop him." His fierceness evaporated as he placed the pistol on the deck and kicked it toward the naked man. "What is it you want?"

"Trade," the man repeated, flicking his chin toward the knife in Fiona's hand.

Her baby for a pocketknife? It was the best deal she'd been offered all day. "Why sure! No problem." She laid the knife on the deck and slid it toward him the way Colin had done the gun. The two lay side-by-side at the man's feet, and Fiona wondered which he would take.

"Ara!"

The gut-wrenching sob made Fiona look to the water. A beautiful woman now clung to the net just outside where the pup had ceased to struggle—the same spot where an adult seal had been only moments before. Her long black hair floated like a shroud around her.

She looked to the boat and screamed something unintelligible to Fiona, something that started and ended with what sounded like, "Dad, seek!"

Fiona turned back to the man. "Who are you people?" But the stranger was already hurdling over the railing.

"Seamus!" Fiona screamed. She was nearly over the side after the kidnapper when a little voice stopped her.

"Eely!" The toddler had been plunked into a puddle mid-deck, far from the boat's edge. This was a very considerate thing for a child thief to do, Fiona thought, as she struggled to catch her breath.

Seamus clambered to unsteady legs and started after the man, but Colin and Fiona converged on him, scooping him into a tight group hug.

By the time they'd recovered their senses enough to turn back to the net, the last of the herring had escaped through a fresh-cut hole. The woman was gone, and so was the pup, not to mention the strange man, who Fiona now thought might have been a figment of her imagination. No one could be that beautiful.

"Eely," Seamus mumbled. He pressed his head to Fiona's chest, stuffed a thumb in his mouth, and gazed out to sea with a look of pure contentment.

"Huh. Will you look at that," Colin said.

He wasn't watching three seals swimming side-by-side into the distance the way Seamus was. Instead, his attention had been drawn to a pocketknife lying neatly folded on the deck.

Chapter 3:
For Want of Flour

Exhausted from helping unload the latest shipping vessel, Oluva collapsed on the country store's porch swing. It was spring on Lítill Vanta Island, the finest season in the North Atlantic. Despite this, sweat dripped from her brow as if it were summer in the Sahara.

Or so she supposed. This oversized rock in the middle of the ocean was all she knew. She'd not been more than these few kilometers south of the Arctic Circle in all her sixteen years.

Oluva and her mother ran Morgan's Market,

the only place on the island where folks could buy food and dry goods, and they'd just pushed twelve cartloads each up the cliff-path from the pier. This was half again the usual haul, and not because it was an extra-large delivery. The problem was little Seamus.

Oluva certainly hadn't gone looking for a summer babysitting job on top of helping her mother in the market. But Mrs. Rafferty, Fiona, had come back from fishing with her husband a couple of weeks before, white as a spring lamb, with no fish to sell in the store.

She'd foisted the toddler into Oluva's arms, saying, "I need a child-minder. You up for it? Good. I'll pay what I can from our haul."

There was some story about a seal pup with a heart-shaped scar and Seamus nearly toppling overboard. Oluva didn't quite get it all, but how could she say no, what with that little rascal scaring the life out of his mama by nearly drowning? So, Oluva accepted the job.

And she was coming to regret it. Seamus had taken up half of her handcart for every load that day, and in his excitement, he would not sit still. He jostled from side to side, peering over the edge, nearly toppling the cart at every turn.

He was giving her a rest just then as he poked the grass with a sharp stick, looking for worms. Oluva's mother was inside double-checking the official list of goods received against what they'd actually gotten—all the merchandise needed to keep the village running until next month's delivery. Maybe longer if storms prevented the ship from coming on schedule.

"Loova look!" Seamus swaggered over, holding a shiny beetle that clambered over his outstretched fingers.

She tousled his rusty curls. "Oluva's tired, sweet-buns. Why don't you chase some hop-grassers for a bit."

He was a sweet little nature buff, and she loved him already, but this was way more work than she'd counted on. Her mother had warned her it'd be tough, but she was sixteen; you couldn't tell her much.

The beetle flew off, abandoning Seamus to seek other delights. So he came over to smoosh Oluva's cheeks into a kissy face as he suggested, "Trot trot to London?"

Why had she ever thought it was a good idea to introduce him to that silly game? "Oh, Shaymie, not now," she moaned, her back throbbing.

"Ahem." Her mother leaned against the door frame, looking as tired as Oluva felt. "Did you remember to order the flour?"

"Of course," she said. But how could she possibly remember what she'd typed into the computer a week ago? Surely, she'd ordered the flour, though. They always ordered flour. Fifty kilos every month. The village baker took forty for bread and pastries, most of which he brought back to sell at the market. The rest they sold in sacks for folks to cook with at home.

Her mother flipped through the pages on her clipboard. "Well, it's not here," she said,

Oluva straightened Seamus on her lap. "I meant to."

"Meant to doesn't feed the town." Her glance rested on Seamus for a moment, the cause of Oluva's distractedness these days. Then she turned and disappeared inside.

"Shit," Oluva said, her knee bouncing of its own accord.

"Shee-it!" Seamus said with the same unbridled exuberance he showed for absolutely everything.

"No, no, Shaymie." She pressed a finger to his lips. "Oh, God, not that."

"Oh, gud, no tat," he repeated, eyes twinkling.

She spun him around so he wouldn't see her smile. Holding him by the armpits, legs straddling her knees, she began:

"Trot trot to London. Trot to Berlin. Lookout, Seamus. Don't fall in!" She dropped him a short half-fall between her knees before lifting him back into riding position.

"Again!" he shouted, and she obliged, thinking maybe she could jostle the 'sh' word out of his little sponge-brain before he imitated her curse to his parents.

Her mother came out on the fourth encore, wearing her rubberized sea-coat. "They've got flour on Groté Vanta," she said. "It'll cost a little more, but we're nearly out, so I'd better boat on over." She fished around in the mailbag she used for a purse and pulled out a set of keys. "Hold down the fort."

"I'm so sorry," Oluva said as her mother headed around back to where the cliff path led down to the dock.

"Shit happens." Her mother waved over her shoulder.

"Shee-it tappinz!" Seamus giggled and waved back.

***

Oluva's mother was still not back by the time Fiona and Colin arrived to pick up their son. "No fish to sell you today," Colin said as he headed for the beer cooler.

Oluva checked the wall clock—still early afternoon. "Giving up so soon?"

Fiona picked up her toddler and swept him skyward, then scooped him into a snuggle. "The Weather Service says a pop-up storm is brewing," she said. "No use taking chances. Right, pumpkin?" She poked the belly button peeking out from under his T-shirt.

"Storm?" Oluva's heart stilled, then recovered in a series of stuttering thumps as she grabbed for the radio transmitter under the counter by the cash register.

"Something wrong?" Fiona asked.

"It's just... Mother is out there."

"In the boat?" Fiona looked to Colin, whose beer had stalled to hang in front of his lips.

"She'll be fine," Colin said, but the two of them made no move to leave, watching and waiting for Oluva to make the call.

Why hadn't her mother turned on the receiver in the store before she left? She might have tried to call, and Oluva wouldn't have known. She flipped the power switch and made sure it was tuned to her mother's frequency. Pressing the TALK button, she said, "Mama Bear. This is Olive Pit. Come in."

She let loose of the button and listened, but there was only static.

"Cute call signs." Fiona grinned, but her

smile faded as the silence dragged on.

Oluva told herself she was overreacting, but herself wasn't buying it. And when the sky out the plate glass window darkened, her panic ratcheted up six notches. Her father had abandoned them before she was born. Mother was all she had.

"Mama Bear," she said, louder this time. "This is Olive Pit. Come in!"

Colin set his beer on the counter and reached to take the radio. "I'll call up the Sea Guard," he said. "They'll send a rescue boat to find her. She was headed for Groté Vanta, I take it?"

Oluva nodded, but she clenched the radio tighter. The big island wasn't that far off, an hour each way. In good weather, anyway.

"She'll answer," Oluva said. "Give her a minute." But all they heard was the rising wind starting to howl around the front awning.

Oluva pressed TALK and repeated her plea. No answer over the radio. But somehow, she heard her mother's voice loud and clear.

"Mama?" Oluva looked over her shoulder to where the woman should be coming in from the back door. But she wasn't.

Colin stood at the counter, searching the directory for a call number. Fiona studied her, rocking Seamus on her hip in an unending series of figure eights. Even the little guy had gone serious. But Oluva was the only one who seemed to hear her mother's cries.

Oh God, oh God, oh God! It was Mama's voice alright, but from where?

Oluva passed the handpiece off to Colin and followed the screams out the rear door that opened into the storeroom. She checked all the aisles between ceiling-high shelves. But Mama wasn't there.

So she followed the curses out onto the cliff-path. As they grew more frantic, the words became clearer. It was as if the wind carried her mother's voice to her from across the sea.

A sheepdog on the nearby hill gathered his flock, herding them to shelter from the storm. He and his charges, heads bowed before the rain, were as oblivious to the screams as Colin, Fiona, and little Seamus had been.

When Mama began to pray the Our Father, Oluva bolted down the hill. Mrs. Morgan was not the praying sort.

"Mama!" Oluva yelled, racing through the narrow switchbacks.

By the time she reached the end of the pier, wind-driven rain pelted her face, and waves slammed against the dock. She shouldn't have been able to hear anything above the roar of the storm, but her mother's voice played on in her head. When she moved on to the Hail Mary, Oluva knew things were bad.

The only reason Oluva knew the Hail Mary was that, in rebellion against Reverend Lockheart's patriarchal elitism, Mrs. Morgan had posted it over the condoms in the back corner. Oluva had thought it hilarious.

Hoping their past irreverence wouldn't count against them, Oluva fell to her knees to pray along with her mother. When they got to the end, though, her mother changed it.

"Holy Mary, mother of God," she said. "Pray for this sinner. Now!" She paused for a long time before adding so quietly Oluva almost didn't hear, "At the hour of my death. Amen."

"Mama, no!" Oluva shouted into the gale. "That's not how it goes!" The deluge diluted her tears but not her grief. "It's 'Pray for US sinners, now *AND* at the hour of *OUR* death'! Not you. Not now!"

But her mother had fallen forever silent.

***

Those were not the first death cries Oluva heard, just the first she recognized for what they were. Her mother's voice in her head that day made it clear just how different she was from the rest of the villagers, and their reactions drove home the point.

A fisherman tying off his boat that afternoon circulated the story of how she'd shouted and cursed at the very moment her mother must have been drowning miles out to sea. From then on, doubt shadowed every face coming to offer condolences or pick up milk and bread from the market.

'Had Oluva caused her mother's death?' they seemed to say. 'Sent her off in that storm? Sabotaged her boat, even?' People could be so cruel, if only in Oluva's mind.

Over the next few days, more stories surfaced, reminding folks of why they'd never quite warmed up to that odd Oluva Morgan. One in particular chilled even Oluva herself. She remembered it vividly.

Pregnant Mrs. Chatham standing in the market, a toddler on her hip. Oluva, about three, running up to her in full sob. She remembered pressing her face to the woman's watermelon belly, weeping. "Poor baby. Poor baby, don't cry."

The adults stood stunned for so long that the front of Mrs. Chatham's dress was soaked with tears and drivel by the time Oluva's mother pulled her away. Her mother had taken her behind the counter to soothe, but she could not be consoled. Oluva was confused and angry that everyone was just standing around while that poor baby wailed in pain.

But they understood soon enough—when Mrs. Chatham doubled over, dropping both a carton of chocolate milk and her toddler. And blood streamed down her leg to fill her shoe.

No, Oluva's mother's weren't the first death cries she'd heard, just the first she fully understood. Nowadays, she knew them all. If anyone died on either of the Vanta Islands, friend or foe, stranger or kin, quickly or over many long, miserable days, Oluva heard their agony.

Occasionally, she found the means to save one. But more often, the Grim Reaper got what he came for.

Chapter 4:
Seamus Sails

Seamus was twelve before his parents allowed him aboard their commercial fishing boat for the first time. At least that's the way he remembered it. Oluva says he used to go out on the *Seabreeze* with his folks every day from the time he was born until about a week before his second birthday.

What changed so suddenly she couldn't say for sure. They'd come back that day with empty nets and shell-shocked faces, mumbling something about nearly losing their sweet bairn to the sea.

Seamus might have thought Oluva was withholding information, except he knew she never would. Though she was fourteen years his elder and hired as his child-minder, the two of them were thick as thieves, her with no mum or da, him with parents out fishing from dawn to dusk, weather permitting. At times it felt like all they had was each other. Until Yurgan came along, and then there were three. But that's another story.

Seamus's parents, though? They knew what had driven them to set their young son ashore, and they weren't talking. He'd given up asking as it seemed only to make them uncomfortable. But he would never quit pushing to join them on their daily fishing excursions. How could a person be expected to live on a ruddy island, especially one as runty as Lítill Vanta, and never be allowed to set sail on the sea?

Mornings when he wasn't in school, he went to the dock with them, ostensibly to help carry nets and gear. In truth, he was angling his way aboard, showing his folks what a boon it would be to have two extra hands shipboard. But always, he ended up standing on the pier, dejected, watching them motor off into the sunrise.

The sea was in his blood, dammit. He'd read every book about the ocean that he could get his hands on. He'd pined over pictures on the internet till his eyes blurred. He was the son of a son of a fisherman, and if he stayed landlocked much longer, it was sure to kill him.

"Please. I'm not that hare-brained baby anymore," he argued. The words had become a morning invocation, for what little good they did. "I won't fall overboard, I swear," he said, tossing the net into the boat with a thud that echoed through the hull louder than it really should have.

"Okay." Da ticked his head to one side, casual-like, as if he agreed to bring his son aboard nine days out of ten instead of… well, never.

Seamus's jaw dropped nearly to the deck. "I can? I can come?"

"Colin, no!" Mum said. "We agreed."

"Be sensible, Fiona." Da took her by the shoulders and lowered his chin to look into her eyes. "You've seen what he and Yurgan are doing while we're gone every day. They're rehabbing that old wreck of a *Kópakonan*. Do you seriously think it'd be better for him to sneak off in that leaky little currach with no knowledge of the sea?" His eyebrows ticked up like hands in prayer, and Seamus smiled to see Da on his side for once.

"We have to teach him, so he'll be safe." Da turned those hopeful eyebrows on Seamus. "Safer anyway."

Mum's fists clenched at her sides. "Okay," she said grudgingly. "But anything happens to him, it's on you."

"You hear that, lad?" Da let loose of Mum and led the way up the ramp onto the *Seabreeze*. "Any trouble from you, and I'm in deep kefir!"

Digging into the storage box under a bench seat, he pulled out a bright orange abomination with armholes. A life vest. "You'll wear this at all times," he said, shoving it at Seamus.

Yurgan watched them from shore as he always did, waiting for Seamus to shuffle back all mopey so they could spend the rest of the day mucking about together. Even from this distance, Seamus could see the shock on his friend's face. Followed in closely by a green wave of envy.

Seamus knew he wasn't the only one yearning for open water, and it hurt him to leave his friend behind. Maybe once he convinced his folks he was no trouble, they could invite Yurgan along, too.

As he slipped into the grotesque orange float-coat, he half expected Yurgan to double over laughing. Instead, his friend flipped him a bird, turned his back, and slumped away. Seamus vowed he would make it up to him. Somehow.

Da was keen to put his new crewmate to

work, teach him everything that first day. Casting off was nothing new for Seamus. He'd often released the tie-line from the pier cleat. The only difference this time was his giddy leap aboard as the boat slipped away from the dock.

Mum took the wheel while Da explained the net and the motorized lift that would haul it aboard filled with their catch, luck permitting. He showed Seamus the proper way to coil ropes and fold the net so it would feed out smoothly when the time came. Then he gave his son a rundown on the radio and who to call in an emergency. Da seemed almost euphoric, like he'd been wanting to share this with his only child for ages and was glad the time had finally come.

"Let's take him over to Stealth Stone," Da said.

Mum scowled. "We haven't found fish out there in months."

"Just a swing-by," Da said. "Show the boy where it's at, so it doesn't take him by surprise." He turned to Seamus. "The damned thing is hard to spot at high tide and can take out your hull before you know what hit you. Well, what you hit, actually." He chuckled.

Da was enjoying himself so much that even Mum had loosened up. She checked the tide chart taped to the instrument panel. "It's even neap tide." When Seamus peered over her shoulder, she explained, "The lowest of the low, right about now."

Da grinned. "That rock should be rising up like a zit on prom night."

"Colin!" Mum shook her head in disgust but veered to starboard and headed around the island. Before long, Seamus spotted a low mound looming up out of the undulating sea.

"Thar she blows!" Da shouted.

Seamus groaned. "More like a turtle than a whale, I'd say." He might not be an experienced mariner, but he knew that much.

"So, now you've seen it." Mum steered the boat back to her original course. "The GPS marks it too, for those days when it's underwater or hidden in fog."

"Hold up." Da took the wheel and steered them back toward the rock. "There's a fair number of birds out there. That could mean a fair number of fish."

As they got closer, the rock seemed to grow lumps all over its back. Seamus eventually identified them as seals. At least a dozen of them.

Mum saw them too. "Colin, let's just go." Her shoulders stiffened as she reached to take the wheel, but Da held tight.

"It's okay," he said so calmly it made the hair

stand up on the back of Seamus's neck. He looked between his parents, trying to decipher the message that passed between them, but they'd had his whole life to develop this secret language that excluded all others.

Da gently pried her fingers from the wheel, all the time looking into her eyes like she was a wild animal about to bolt. "There might be a school of herring over there, and we can't afford to pass up that chance."

She backed away to sit in the copilot's seat, but her eyes stayed fixed on the ever-nearing rock and the seals that sprawled over it.

"What are they doing?" Seamus whispered like he would have in church, though he couldn't think why.

"Hauled out to rest, I'd guess." Da slowed the motor as they drew near. "Probably full up on the fish that must be around here somewhere." He scanned the waters around them, so Seamus did the same, but there didn't seem to be any fish.

"There's a dead one," Mum said in a pinched voice. Her eyes were still on the rock. "Let's just go, Colin. Please."

Sure enough. Draped at the high center of the stone was the body of a dead seal, the biggest one Seamus had ever seen. Admittedly his experience was limited to those that came to the island, but this one was huge. It had a massive forehead hump to match, which, according to his reading, marked it as an old bull, probably the leader of this pod. Well, used to be, anyway. His subjects were arranged in a circle around him, heads bowed in the direction of the deceased.

It's a funeral, Seamus thought. They'd stumbled on a ruddy seal funeral! How cool was that?

As though hearing Seamus's irreverent thoughts, the biggest of the living seals lifted its head and glared at him. The forehead on the brute indicated that he was likely next in line to be leader of the pack. And he didn't look pleased with the intrusion on this solemn ceremony.

"Maybe Mum's right," Seamus said. "We should leave them to whatever this is."

At the sound of Seamus's voice, one of the smaller seals, not a pup but not full-grown, looked up. It locked eyes with him, lifted its nose to the breeze, and sniffed. Its whiskers twitched as it inched toward the water, slipped in, and slid through the waves toward the *Seabreeze*.

Seamus moved to the side of the boat for a closer look. "Hi there," he said, and the bark in reply was so friendly he grinned like a fool.

"Hey! It likes me!" He turned to find his parents staring, slack jawed.

A string of loud, angry growls from the rock pulled his attention back. The presumptive new leader was charging. The big guy made such a splash that it drenched the rock and three of its occupants.

He was fast in the water, too. Before Seamus could think what was happening, the big bull was at the side of the boat. He grabbed the smaller seal in his teeth and dragged it away by the scruff of its neck like a puppy. Apparently, he didn't like the little one fraternizing with humans.

At the rock's edge, the bully shoved the underling up to join the others. His final push folded its tail flukes sharply, maybe painfully, and a flash of white on the black underside caught the sun.

"Eely!" Mum gasped. Her face had gone as pale as bleached whalebones washed up on shore. Da whipped the boat around and roared out to sea without a word.

Seamus's folks were silent and somber the rest of the day. He hadn't a clue why their mood had shifted so swiftly, but they seemed to go out of their way to frame every task as drudge work that no kid in his right mind would volunteer for.

The looks that passed between them in that secret language spoke louder than words. They regretted bringing him, but why? He'd done everything they asked and more. And he hadn't even come close to falling overboard.

"You can't keep me stuck on land, you know," he said as they heaped the day's haul into handcarts destined for Morgan's Market. "One way or another, I'm going to sea. With or without your permission."

The next look Da sent Mum included those prayer eyebrows from earlier. She closed her eyes and let out a breath of resignation.

"We'd best order his waxed jacket tonight," she said. "The nor'easters will be blasting before you know it, and we can't get much work out of him if he's half-froze."

Seamus's heart nearly burst. Finally, his time had come.

The rest of that summer and into fall, he kept an eye out for that friendly little seal. By the following spring, he'd forgotten all about her. Again.

Chapter 5:
The King's Tales

Beneath the grandest Scallop Moon of summer, King Tatzeek of the Selkies led his pod from the open ocean to Whalebone Beach. The dozen or so seals dipped and bobbed silently up a ribbon of moonlight past rocky cliffs to the black sand beach.

Wait here, said the king, his silent thought-command passing through the pod, and the seal folk did as they were bid. They milled in the waves offshore as he hauled out to survey the land. He sniffed and scanned, then closed his eyes and listened hard with ears as well as his sixth sense—telepathy to hear the thoughts of others: Selkies, beasts, and sometimes humans.

All was calm and tranquil so far as he could tell. So, he let his sealskin part at the seam down his nose. When it slid away to reveal his human face, a mane of thick, black hair tumbled to his shoulders. His tanned cheekbones seemed carved from stone, and his keen black eyes shone like polished coal. Rising to his feet, he let the sealskin fall from a frame that rivaled gods of humankind. But he was neither god nor human.

He was Selkie.

Tucking his sealskin under one arm, he strode the beach from end to end, insuring his people would be safe from prying eyes and thieving men. Finally, he called his clan ashore.

One by one, the seal folk came, inching up the beach and spreading out across the sand. As the Selkies shed their pelts of fine soft fur, more gods and goddesses materialized to strut and sway upon the sand, each more beautiful than the last. Restrained until now, they began to hum and sing and raise their arms to the stars, basking in the warm salt air.

Silence! The king sent his command from mind to mind, and all the folk obeyed. *You must attend to The Solemn Selkie History before our revelries begin.*

Oh, Father. Not that tired tale, a young girl said.

She hardened her face and puffed her chest, mimicking her father's lecture stance. *Many million moons ago,* she recited formally, *five careless Selkie maidens came to shore. They left their sealskins in a pile to frolic in their women's forms beneath the starlit skies. They formed a circle holding hands and reveled till the break of dawn. But when time came to go back home, only four of their sealskins could be found. The last was clutched in human hands, never to be free again.*

She shook her head till her black hair rippled. *Then it goes on about how that wicked fisherman kept her captive until she finally died, and it was such a blessing because who would want to live on land like a human anyway. We all know every word by heart, Father.*

Several in the crowd nodded.

And it happened so long ago, back when humans actually knew we existed. We're safe from them now. You worry too much.

The people held their breaths, fearing the king might grow so angry at his insolent daughter he would cancel the night's festivities.

Instead, he said, *Alright, Ara. I have another tale. This one from a time when I was about your age, and I too thought I knew everything.*

Murmuring with excitement at a brand-new story, the seal folk settled down to listen. They perched on driftwood or rested in the sand, lounging against one another in relaxed companionship.

This should be good, said Ara, pulling her small sister to her lap and combing fingers through the little one's auburn hair.

Hmph, said the king. *I've never thought it so.*

He ran his gaze over the people, then over their heads and out to sea. *Once, not so very long ago,* he began, *there was a Selkie girl much like you or you.* He pointed to his daughters each in turn. *She believed herself quite wise, but she was not so clever as she thought.*

What was her name? Ara said, looking up from braiding her sister's tresses.

Laksani. And she was the most beautiful of us all. His face slackened at the memory. *Like you—* he waved both arms to embrace all his people—*she loved skin-shed nights under a golden Scallop Moon. She loved them more than anything and was always the first to take on her human form and the last to return to seal-shape at the king's command.*

But not you, right?

Ara, please. You know I wasn't king when I was your age. Hush now, so we can get on to the celebrations.

There was a rustling of agreement, so Ara bent back to her sister's hair.

Laksani, the king continued, *so loved her human form that she began to sneak off by herself on dark Splinter-Moon nights. And even near-black No-Moon nights. She bragged to us how fine it was to sing and dance in human form without the elders insisting on traditional style and tempo. She begged all the youths to come along, but none of us was quite so foolish.* His broad shoulders sagged a little. *Nor were we brave enough to tell the king so he might save Laksani from herself.*

Oh, at first, she was cautious. She promised she would make sure the beach was empty and hide her sealskin underneath a heavy rock. But as time went on, she grew more lax.

On the night that she was taken, so she told me later, she'd gone to a beach she'd been to many times before and so considered safe. 'No one ever goes there,' she said. 'Least of all a human, especially on these darkest nights.' So, she had no doubt the empty strand would be hers and hers alone.

But a man was *there. He watched the seal Laksani swim ashore with little interest. And had she stayed a seal, he'd have thought no more about it. But, of course, she didn't. She bared her woman form to the night sky, sang in her sonorous voice, and whirled and danced across the sand, graceful as a gull in flight.*

Of course, the weak-willed man was lost under the spell she hadn't even known she'd cast. Laksani didn't see him until he was upon her. He took her hand and held it tight, rambling of his love for her, so deep he could not imagine life alone. A simple human with limited intelligence, he couldn't understand that this was just her Selkie spell turning his brain to mush.

The king looked to each of his subjects, saving a long final stare for his rebellious daughter's eyes. *He could not know that he was caught up in a curse our Selkie kind have suffered since time itself began. And Laksani had no way to explain it to him.*

That infatuated sponge-skull understood only one thing. It didn't take an agile porpoise brain to reason out that, without her sealskin, Laksani could not flee from him. So, he grabbed up the skin that he had watched her hide. He put it in a box which he sat upon till morning, all the while professing his great, enduring love for the girl he'd resolved to abduct against her will.

At sunrise, a boat bigger than any Laksani had ever seen came and took them both away. He said to call him Radcliff and bade her drape herself in man-made cover that scratched her skin to redness, and the boat he called a yacht carried her many days from home.

The elders moaned, and Ara's eyes grew as round as the moon now high above them.

The king went on.

Once off the boat, Radcliff took her to a metal hulk on land that he called his limousine. *It took them to where his* private jet *awaited. This flying thing took them high above the clouds, and after many hours brought them down to a place so dry that her fragile human skin seemed about to crackle off. She wondered what other form might lay beneath this human one she had quickly grown to detest. But there was nothing new for her to become.*

By the time Radcliff let her rest, she was locked inside a box so huge she could not see the sky. When she begged for home, he told her she would grow to love his ugly mansion, *and it would be her home forever.*

But it wasn't? Ara dared to whisper. *Laksani told you this story, so she must have come back?*

For a bit, the king agreed. *Laksani lived with Radcliff as what humans call a wife. She bore him a son and three small daughters, and all this time, he spoke of his love and adoration but refused to give her back her skin.*

He forced her to wear chains around her neck and jewels that stabbed into her earflaps. He gave her clothing, stiff and binding, and shoes that pinched her feet. Worst of all, he insisted she eat his strange exotic foodstuff. All she craved was uncooked fish or crab, but he forced her to eat pastries, wines, and pasta until her stomach rebelled and sent them back to him in ways that did not please him.

One listener groaned in horror. *Oh, dear Titan!* Another turned away to retch.

There were two foods he gave her, though, that she could tolerate—raw oysters and Russian caviar. Still, she grew weak after years on only these. It seems her curse did, too, for day by day, Radcliff loosened his tight hold on her.

He returned her to us, finally, just a shell of the woman she had been. It was only luck that migration placed our pod in the selfsame fishing grounds Radcliff had taken her from six earth-turns before.

He brought her in his yacht to that very beach, gave her back her skin, and sailed away as though he'd no more use for her. As though he felt no shame at the horror he had done.

I watched him go, then raced to where Laksani lay, weak as a newborn pup. She died a half moon-cycle later.

The joyous mood had fled. Without a sound, the seal folk donned their skins and slipped one by one into the sea, until only Ara and her father remained. She'd never seen him look so beaten.

I didn't know, she said, regretting having pushed him to relive those awful times.

He took her hand. *It's a hard one to tell*, he said, *but you must promise me you'll take this tale to heart. We are not so safe as you would like to think.*

She nodded. But she was young, and real understanding wouldn't come for her until much later.

Author's Note

If you enjoyed *Ara's Prelude*, you might like to continue the saga in *Ara's Song*. Also, it would greatly help the author for you to leave a review wherever you bought this book.

Other books by D. August Baertlein

Ara's Song (The Selkie Chronicles)—The further adventures of Ara, Seamus, Oluva, and others. (Available in eBook and paperback, and soon to be in audio.)

Synapse—Brain research thriller. (Available in eBook and paperback.)

About the Author

D. August Baertlein was sure she'd be a marine ecologist, and she's never lost her love of the sea. But a multitude of interests drove her to transfer to genetics for her doctorate. Perhaps she thought to clone herself into enough copies to do it all.

When the cloning thing didn't work out, she took up computer programming to pay the bills. Now she wanders the high chaparral around her home and dreams up stories. Every creature she meets sparks her imagination and quickens her heart. A startled rattlesnake or nosy mountain lion can send her pulse rate skyrocketing.

She drifts around social media as DAugustBaertlein and occasionally blogs at www.daugustbaertlein.com.

Photo By Radford Davis

97718133R10042